Leprechauns
Don't Play
Basketball

Leprechauns Don't Play Basketball

by Debbie Dadey
and
Marcia Thornton Jones

illustrated by John Steven Gurney

A
LITTLE APPLE
PAPERBACK

SCHOLASTIC INC.

New York   Toronto   London   Auckland   Sydney

ISBN 0-590-44822-6

25 24 23 22 21 20   7 8 9/9 0/0

Printed in the U.S.A.   40

First Scholastic printing, February 1992

To Mandy, Kevin, and Damon — D.D.
To Barbara and Lee — M.T.J.

Contents

1

Mean Green Pinching Machine

Melody and Liza met on the playground under the budding oak tree. The girls always met there before school. They were so busy giggling that neither one saw Eddie sneaking up behind them. He was wearing a Kelly green T-shirt under his blue jacket, and a green baseball cap. Eddie reached around the gnarled tree trunk and pinched Melody as hard as he could.

"Ow!" screeched Melody. "Why'd you do that?"

"You're not wearing green," Eddie said. "Everybody knows that if you don't wear green on Saint Patrick's Day you get pinched. And I'm a mean green pinching machine."

"Well," Melody snapped, "for your information, I am wearing green!"

"Where?" Eddie asked

Melody pointed to her tennis shoes. Each one was tied with a bright green shoelace. "I get to pinch you back," Melody insisted as she reached out to get him.

Eddie raced across the playground and barreled into the third-grade classroom of Bailey Elementary to have some St. Patrick's Day fun. But first, he glanced around to be sure that Mrs. Jeepers wasn't in the room.

His teacher, Mrs. Jeepers, had long red hair and eyes the color of lime Kool-Aid.

She always wore a giant brooch that matched her eyes. Mrs. Jeepers didn't allow any shenanigans. If someone tried to cause trouble, she would flash her green eyes in that student's direction and rub the brooch at her neck. There was something strange about her—very strange. Some kids even thought she was a vampire. After all, she was from the Transylvanian Alps in Romania where Count Dracula had lived. She even wore a bat bracelet, which was definitely not normal for a teacher. The third-graders in Mrs. Jeepers' room didn't dare make her mad.

Luckily, Mrs. Jeepers was nowhere to be seen. Eddie sneaked up behind Carey, the teacher's pet. She always got to school early to clean the chalkboards. Just as he had suspected, there wasn't a stitch of green on her. Eddie reached out to pinch her, but he never got the chance.

"Eddie, I am surprised to see you so

early." Goose bumps ran wild all over Eddie's arms and neck when he heard Mrs. Jeepers speak in her strange accent.

Eddie and Carey both turned to face their teacher. Mrs. Jeepers stood in the door. She wore a purple skirt that touched the tops of her black pointy boots, and her brooch was pinned to the collar of her starched white shirt. She smiled at Eddie with an odd little half smile.

"I . . . I . . . I just thought I'd play a leprechaun trick," Eddie stammered.

Mrs. Jeepers stopped smiling and she rubbed the brooch at her neck. "I will not allow activities having to do with those creatures." She shook her finger at Eddie.

Eddie blinked in surprise. "But it's just for fun. And besides, there isn't really any such thing as a leprechaun."

"Wouldn't it be neat if there were some leprechauns around here?" Carey giggled.

"*No!*" Mrs. Jeepers gasped. "Where I come from leprechauns are considered worse than blood-sucking mosquitoes."

"But why?" Carey asked. "They're so cute in pictures."

"Ahh, but the true leprechaun is not as you imagine," Mrs. Jeepers whispered. "Their mischievous tricks are a nuisance the world can do without."

Eddie wanted to ask more about leprechauns, but the bell rang to start school. As the rest of the class filed in the door, Eddie couldn't help wondering why Mrs. Jeepers didn't like leprechauns.

2

Eddie Cuts Loose

Eddie slammed his math book shut and looked around the third-grade classroom. Kids were bending over their books like they were performing heart surgery. He'd been working hard all morning, too. As a matter of fact, he'd been working hard ever since Mrs. Jeepers came to Bailey Elementary. Eddie scratched his curly red hair and watched the second hand of the clock sweep around. He tapped his pencil as each second passed.

"Shhhh," Howie hissed.

Eddie stuck out his tongue at the freckled face of his best friend. But he did stop tapping his pencil when Mrs. Jeepers flashed her eyes in his direction.

Eddie felt around inside his desk for something to do. He dug through wrinkled scraps of paper stuck to old bubble-gum wads, pencils without erasers, a pile of dried glue, broken crayons, dried-up markers, old test papers with F's, Howie's missing baseball card, and a pair of scissors. Eddie hooked his fingers into the scissors. He snipped a few of the F's off his old test papers and stuck them to a wad of bubble gum. It was then that he noticed how one long strand of Liza's hair had fallen out of her ponytail. The long clump was dangling right on Eddie's desk.

Eddie glanced up at Mrs. Jeepers. Luckily, she was busy helping Carey. He grinned wickedly and inched the scissors across his desk. Very slowly, he surrounded the hair with the sharp metal scissors. One snip and the deed would be done.

Eddie squeezed like he was pulling the trigger of a gun. But something was wrong. The scissors wouldn't close. Eddie squeezed harder but it was like they were frozen. It was then that he saw a green flash in the front of the room. Eddie gulped as Mrs. Jeepers rubbed the green brooch at her neck and smiled her odd little half smile.

Caught again, Eddie thought to himself as he put away his scissors. He never could have any fun in Mrs. Jeepers' room.

But it was almost time for gym. Gym was the one time he could really cut loose. All that basketball dribbling must have turned Coach Ellison's brains to mashed potatoes because he never knew what was going on.

Finally, Mrs. Jeepers stood up from her desk. "It is time for physical education," she said in her strange Romanian accent. "Please line up."

Every time Mrs. Jeepers spoke, Eddie got goose bumps. Her accent reminded him of a Dracula movie he'd seen. Eddie joined the rest of the class in line. As soon as his teacher turned away he pinched Liza's chubby arm.

"*Ow!*" Liza screeched. She slapped her hand over her mouth just as Mrs. Jeepers turned around.

"Is there something the matter?" Mrs. Jeepers asked Liza.

"N-n-no, ma'am," Liza stuttered.

Eddie snickered as they walked down the hall. "Scaredy-cat," he whispered to Liza.

Liza did her best to ignore Eddie. Everybody did their best to ignore him. But Eddie was itching for some excitement. By the time the class had reached the bathrooms, he had managed to pinch three people, trip two, and kick another.

But that wasn't enough for Eddie. Unfortunately for Howie, the girls' bathroom door was propped open. Eddie acted fast before he missed his chance. He grabbed Howie and pushed him into the girls' bathroom. The girls giggled as Howie stumbled out.

"What's wrong with you?" Howie whispered. "Are you trying to get in trouble?"

"No," Eddie admitted slyly. "I just want to have a little Saint Patrick's Day fun."

"You'd better watch out or Mrs. Jeepers will turn you into bat bait," Howie warned. "Then you'll be sorry."

Eddie's face grew pale. One time he

made Mrs. Jeepers so mad she dragged him out in the hall. The way her green eyes flashed and the warning she hissed had made the blood drain from his face. He never admitted to anyone what had happened in the hall, but the thought of it was enough to keep him quiet, at least until he got to the gym.

3

Mr. Potato Head

In the gym a very short man wearing a red sweat suit and green high-top tennis shoes stood beside their gym teacher. The stranger was so short he only came up to the waistband of Coach Ellison's pea-green sweat suit. The little man made Coach Ellison look like the Jolly Green Giant.

"Who's the peanut?" Eddie asked Howie. "He looks like something that fell out of Santa's sleigh."

"Yeah," Howie agreed, "and I think he fell on his face."

The boys looked at the tiny man's face. He had more lines on it than watermelons had seeds.

Liza whispered, "I bet he's a million years old."

13

"This guy is definitely a good candidate for a face-lift." Melody giggled.

"Yes," Liza agreed. "But he has a nice smile. He reminds me of my grandpa."

"I bet your grandpa doesn't carry a marble bag." Eddie pointed to a small leather pouch hanging from the stranger's waistband. He knew it was the kind that held marbles.

Coach Ellison interrupted them. "Boys and girls, I'd like to introduce you to Mr. O'Grady. He's a teacher from Ireland."

"Top of the morning, lads and lassies." Mr. O'Grady's eyes darted from face to face.

Coach Ellison slapped Mr. O'Grady on the back. "We're very lucky to have Mr. O'Grady visiting for a few days. He'll be teaching a lesson on Irish folk dancing." With that, Coach Ellison left for the teachers' lounge.

Some of the kids groaned, but not Eddie. "This will be great," he whispered to

Howie. "A brand-new teacher to drive batty."

Howie shook his head. "Mr. O'Grady looks like he's been around the block a few times. He might not be as easy as Coach Ellison."

Eddie laughed. "How much trouble can a man the size of Mr. Potato Head be?"

Just then "Mr. Potato Head" started talking with an Irish accent. "Children, it's delighting me to be your coach and friend."

Mr. O'Grady's voice had a ring to it that sounded like birds singing on a spring morning. But Eddie wasn't bothering to listen. He didn't want to waste precious time listening to a guy who wasn't tall enough to get ice cream out of the freezer.

First, Eddie squeaked his tennis shoes on the wooden floor. It sounded like he'd eaten too many beans. Eddie giggled but no one else seemed to notice. They were too busy listening to the strange-sounding shrimp in the red sweat suit. He was talking about doing a dance. *What a sissy thing*, Eddie thought. Eddie wasn't the least bit interested so he turned his attention to Melody.

She was listening to Mr. O'Grady like he was giving the answers to tomorrow's math test. Quietly, Eddie crept up behind her and tied her green shoestrings together in a double knot. Then he stood back to watch the action.

"Now, let us be a-trying the jig," Mr. O'Grady said. All the third-graders moved to their assigned places. Melody moved, too. But her feet didn't go along.

Ker-plunk! Melody fell on the floor with a thud. "Ohhhh," she wailed as Mr. O'Grady ran up to help her.

"What has happened to this beautiful lassie?" Mr. O'Grady asked.

Melody sniffed and pointed to Eddie. "He made me fall."

"Oh, me lucky charms," Mr. O'Grady smiled. "I did not think I'd be a-finding an imp so quickly."

"He's an imp all right," Melody snarled as she untangled her shoes. "He's always causing trouble."

"Let's not be too hasty to pass judgment on him," Mr. O'Grady said. "Sometimes much can be gained by tricks."

Eddie felt goose bumps cover his arm and neck. He wasn't used to a teacher being cheerful after one of his pranks.

"Gee," Howie whispered as Mr. O'Grady helped Melody off the floor. "He doesn't get mad very easily."

"We'll see about that," Eddie snapped. "If there's one thing I know, it's how to make teachers mad."

But Howie didn't hear Eddie because Mr. O'Grady started the record player. The lilting music of fiddles and flutes filled the gym. Mr. O'Grady put his hands on his hips and started to step to the music. It wasn't long before everybody joined him. Everybody, that is, except Eddie.

4

ing for Dancers

Eddie watched his friends act like grass-hoppers on a trampoline. "There's no way I'm going to hop around like that," he muttered while sneaking behind the bleachers.

There, waiting for Eddie, were enough basketballs to make thirty seals happy. The balls were in two huge string bags. Eddie jerked on the strings and turned the balls loose. With only a little help from Eddie they started rolling straight for the dancers and Mr. O'Grady.

"Bowling for dancers." Eddie giggled as he waited for kids to start falling. But the balls never reached their targets. Instead, they slowed down and stopped. Eddie scratched his head. "What's going on?"

Eddie didn't notice Mr. O'Grady reaching deep into his marble bag as the balls started rolling again. Only this time, they were heading straight for Eddie.

Eddie stepped away from the rolling balls, but they were like magnets. The more he high-stepped, the more the balls bumped against his feet.

"I'm glad to see you are a-joining our happy jig." Mr. O'Grady's voice suddenly came from behind him.

Eddie jumped and banged into the bleachers. He rubbed his head and stuttered. "N-n-ooo. Dancing's for girls."

"To dance is to live," Mr. O'Grady smiled. "My people always are a-dancing. 'Tis the men that love it the most!"

Eddie rolled his eyes. "Then the men are sissies!"

The sound of Mr. O'Grady's laughter matched the music from the record player. "'Tis nothing wrong with liking a good time!"

Eddie couldn't argue with that.

Mr. O'Grady's eyes crinkled with laughter as he continued. "Dancing is one of three ways we folk have fun."

"What are the other two ways?" Eddie asked as he kicked a basketball out of his way.

Mr. O'Grady pulled open his drawstring pouch. "A little dancing and a few more gems in our pouches make us happy as a robin in spring."

Eddie stared at the sparkling stones of different colors in the pouch. "Where did you get those?" he asked.

"That's what I'm a-telling you." Mr. O'Grady laughed as he pulled out a stone the color of a cherry. He rubbed it gently with his thumb. "The folk like to collect stones from around the world."

Eddie stared at the bright gem. "Jewelry is for sissies, too," Eddie finally said. "What's the third thing you do to have fun?"

"'Tis the favorite pastime of the folk," Mr. O'Grady whispered. "But a thing the monsters from Transylvania cannot stand."

Eddie jerked to attention. "What do you know about Transylvania?"

"I know they cannot stand the tricks of the folk," Mr. O'Grady said.

"But Mrs. Jeepers is from the Transylvanian Alps," Eddie blurted. Then he wished he'd kept his mouth shut because Mr. O'Grady's face grew as red as his sweat suit.

"This teacher of yours, would she have hair the color of the sunrise? And be a serious sort who allows no fun-loving shenanigans?"

"Boy, that's for sure," Eddie agreed.

"And would she be wearing a brooch the color of spring grass?" Mr. O'Grady asked.

Eddie's eyes got big as he nodded.

"So she *is* here," Mr. O'Grady chuckled

as he slid the red stone into his pouch and jerked the string tight.

Mr. O'Grady grabbed one of the basketballs and twirled away from Eddie. With-

out another word he zigzagged his way through the dancing third-graders to the record player. The screech of the needle across the record brought the dancers to a halt.

"What's the matter?" Liza asked. "Weren't we doing the dance right?"

Mr. O'Grady smiled. "You dance like butterflies in a field of daisies. But our friend Eddie seems to be a-wanting to play with basketballs instead."

All the kids glared at Eddie, who was still trying to kick away the basketballs.

"But I was having fun dancing," Liza whined.

Melody nodded her head. "Eddie ruins everything."

Mr. O'Grady bounced the ball. "Basketball is a grand way to be having fun, too. Why, back home they call me Magic O'Grady on the court. Let me be a-showing you a few tricks."

The third-graders watched Mr. O'Grady dribble the ball down the center of the court. His little pouch jingled with each step.

"Aw, that's nothing," Eddie sneered as Mr. O'Grady went by. "My kid sister could do that with her eyes closed."

Mr. O'Grady stopped in the middle of the court just long enough to reach into his little pouch.

Suddenly, the ball became an orange blur as Mr. O'Grady whizzed the ball between his legs and around his back. The kids gasped as the little man in the red suit twirled the ball on the tip of one finger. In the next second, he threw the ball all the way down the court. As the ball swished through the net without touching the rim, Mr. O'Grady danced a little jig.

"All right!" Howie clapped and poked Eddie in the ribs.

Eddie watched as the third-graders of Bailey Elementary crowded around the short gym teacher and then he shrugged. "We'll just see how long his Irish luck lasts!"

5

Green Blood

"You'd think we could at least cut out some green shamrocks," Liza complained at the lunch table.

"Maybe we will this afternoon," Melody suggested as she tore open her sandwich bag.

"No." Eddie shook his head. "Mrs. Jeepers doesn't want to have anything to do with Saint Patrick's Day. All because she hates leprechauns."

"What's to hate?" Howie asked. "They're just make-believe creatures."

"Yeah," Liza agreed. "They're cute, too."

"Not according to Mrs. Jeepers," Carey broke in.

"From listening to her, you'd think leprechauns were responsible for the black

28

plague," Eddie said in between bites of an apple.

"She must know something about leprechauns that we don't know," Melody said.

"I'll ask my grandmother to tell me about Saint Patrick's Day and leprechauns," Howie thought out loud. "She's visiting this week and she was born in Ireland."

Melody giggled. "I bet you have green blood. You're probably part leprechaun."

"Just because somebody's from Ireland doesn't mean they're a leprechaun," Howie said. "If that was true Mr. O'Grady would be a leprechaun."

"Well, he is short," Melody pointed out.

"And he does carry a pouch," Liza said. "I bet it's full of gold."

"That's not a pouch for gold," Eddie interrupted. All his friends turned to look at him.

"How do you know?" Melody asked.

Eddie shrugged. "Because he showed me."

"What's in it?" Howie asked.

"Just a bunch of stupid stones," Eddie said as he bit into his chocolate fudge brownie. "He collects them."

Melody gasped. "He *must* be a leprechaun. He's from Ireland, he's short, and he's got a treasure. He probably has a pot of gold hidden somewhere."

"What are you talking about? There's no such thing as leprechauns." Eddie sounded more sure than he felt.

Howie shrugged. "Maybe not. But Mr. O'Grady is no regular coach. I think we better watch out," he said quietly. "Mr. O'Grady is strange. Did you notice how he never looks straight into your eyes?"

"Yeah," Melody agreed. "He looks at your nose instead."

"He may be short," Liza said. "And he may be from Ireland, but I'm pretty sure leprechauns don't play basketball."

Everyone burst out laughing, but they grew silent when Mrs. Jeepers walked over to their table.

"Did I hear the word *leprechaun*?" she demanded.

"No, ma'am," Eddie lied.

"We were just talking about the new coach," Melody told her.

Liza spoke up. "His name is Mr. O'Grady and he's from Ireland. Isn't that neat?"

Mrs. Jeepers's face went ghostly pale and her eyes flashed. "Did you say . . . Ireland?"

Liza nodded. "He loves to dance so he taught us an Irish jig. You'll really like him."

Mrs. Jeepers' green eyes flashed. "I have no desire to meet anyone from Ireland."

"But he's so much fun!" Liza said. "And he collects different kinds of stones! He even showed them to Eddie."

"Shhh," Howie hissed, but it was too late.

Mrs. Jeepers touched her brooch. "So he has found me. I did not think it would be so soon."

With that, Mrs. Jeepers hurried away from the table and out of the cafeteria.

The kids looked at each other. Eddie finally broke the silence. "What did she mean by that?"

Howie shook his head. "I'm not sure. But I think there's going to be trouble."

6

Stairway to the Emerald Isle

That afternoon the four kids met under the oak tree. "I wonder why Mrs. Jeepers acted so strange when we told her about Mr. O'Grady?" Melody asked.

"Maybe he's her long lost husband," Liza said wistfully.

"But she acted scared," Eddie reminded them.

"Maybe her long lost husband is an ax murderer," Melody giggled nervously.

"But Mrs. Jeepers said her husband was dead," Howie pointed out.

"Maybe Mr. O'Grady's with the Irish CIA," Melody suggested. "Mrs. Jeepers might be an international jewel thief."

"Maybe Mr. O'Grady really is a leprechaun," Liza said softly. "You know Mrs. Jeepers doesn't like them."

"Why don't you guys come home with me for a few minutes?" Howie suggested. "My grandmother knows all about Ireland. I'm sure she can tell us about leprechauns. She'll know why Mrs. Jeepers is afraid of them."

"I guess it'd be okay—just for a minute," Melody said.

Everyone else nodded and headed toward Howie's house. It didn't take long for the four friends to walk the three blocks. They dumped their bookbags in the front hall and found Howie's grandmother in the family room, reading the newspaper. Her curly gray hair danced around her head and her eyes sparkled like blue sapphires.

"Well, Howie." His grandmother smiled and put down her newspaper. "You look to be bringing half the school home with you."

Howie introduced Melody, Liza, and Eddie. He was barely finished when Eddie blurted, "We need to know about leprechauns."

Howie's grandmother's smile faded, but just for a moment. "So, Saint Patrick's Day has you a-wondering about the little fairy folk. 'Tis a good thing to talk about on this fine day." His grandmother's voice tinkled with the same accent as Mr. O'Grady's. "Treat yourselves to some cookies and I'll be a-telling you some leprechaun tales."

The kids helped themselves to a handful of cookies from the kitchen and then settled down to listen.

"Once upon a time in Ireland," Howie's grandmother began.

"No, Grandma," Howie interrupted. "We have to have the true story of leprechauns."

Melody nodded. "Our teacher wouldn't tell us a thing."

"Mrs. Jeepers acted very strange today," Howie explained. "She's from Ro-

mania and she won't even talk about leprechauns."

Howie's grandmother frowned. "Saints preserve us," she said quietly. "Leprechauns are a most peculiar fairy folk. Most people don't know the true history of their race."

"But they're just cute little men who wear green and hide pots of gold at the ends of rainbows," Liza said.

"Ah, truth is a rainbow doesn't lead only to a pot of gold," Howie's grandmother whispered. "A rainbow is also a leprechaun's stairway to the Emerald Isle."

"What's the Emerald Isle?" Melody asked.

"'Tis another name for Ireland," Howie's grandmother explained. "Settle back and I'll be a-telling you the true story of the wee folk."

The four kids sat on the floor and peered up at the old woman. She spoke so quietly they had to lean forward to hear.

7

The True Story of the Wee Folk

"Long ago, leprechauns could be found throughout the world," Howie's grandmother began. "The leprechaun emperor ruled the lands by possession of the stolen Fairy Stone. There are many kinds of magic stones—red, blue, and even purple. But the most powerful one of all is the Fairy Stone. It holds a strong magic, the stone does. So powerful, that the leprechauns became a nuisance with it. They traveled the world, tricking anyone they could."

"What was the stone like?" Melody asked.

"The Fairy Stone is as green as the grass underfoot and the trees overhead. And the leprechauns were proud to have it. The emperor wore it at the throat of his scarlet robe."

"Scarlet!" Eddie nearly shouted. "But that's red. Everybody knows leprechauns wear green!"

Howie's grandmother shook her head. "Not in those long-ago times. They only began to wear green when they went into hiding."

"Why did they go into hiding?" Howie asked.

"'Twas the fault of the vampires...."

"*The vampires!*" all four kids yelled at once.

"Aye," Howie's grandmother nodded seriously. "The vampires grew tired of the leprechauns' tricky ways. So they decided to get the Fairy Stone away from the wee folk."

"What happened?" Melody asked. "How did the vampires get the Fairy Stone from the leprechauns?"

"They were tricked!" Howie's grandmother exclaimed. "The vampires sent a spy to live in the emperor's castle. The spy gained their trust and then sneaked

into the emperor's bedroom, taking the Fairy Stone whilst he slept."

"But that's stealing!" Liza cried.

Howie's grandmother shook her head. "The truth of the matter is that the Fairy Stone rightfully belonged to the vampires. And once they got it back, the vampires banished all leprechauns to the Emerald Isle. 'Tis then that leprechauns began to wear green and to hide amongst the trees and bushes. Some say it was because of shame, and to this day most leprechauns of Ireland are too ashamed to look at you. Some say you can control a leprechaun if you get him to look in your eyes."

"But didn't the leprechauns try to get the stone back?" Eddie asked.

"Aye, and they're still a-trying to this day," Howie's grandmother said. "But 'tis only three days that the leprechauns can be a-missing from the Emerald Isle. One day for each leaflet of the shamrock. The vampires saw fit to punish them that way."

"Was it Count Dracula who got the stone back for the vampires?" Eddie asked. "Is that who the emperor trusted?"

Howie's grandmother looked at each one of them. And then she answered in a whisper, "'Twas a teacher that tricked the emperor. The teacher of his very own children!"

The children were silent as they left the room. Out on the front porch Howie whispered. "That's it!"

"What?" Eddie asked.

"Didn't you hear what my grandmother said? A vampire, who just happens to be a teacher, stole the Fairy Stone from the leprechauns."

"So?" Melody shrugged.

"So, the vampire teacher is Mrs. Jeepers," Howie explained, "and she stole the Fairy Stone. You know that weird green brooch she always wears—that's the magic stone. And I bet those stones in Mr. O'Grady's pouch are magic, too."

"You don't know that," Melody insisted. "We don't even know Mrs. Jeepers is a vampire."

"It does sort of fit together," Liza said thoughtfully.

"Of course it does." Howie nodded his head. "And that means Mr. O'Grady really is a leprechaun and he's come to get the stone back."

"That's just a fairy tale," Eddie disagreed. "It's all a bunch of blarney!"

"You won't think so if we have a leprechaun and vampire war right in the halls of Bailey Elementary," Howie said seriously. All the kids were silent as they thought about what he said.

"If that's true," Melody whispered, "we've got to do something to stop it."

"But what can we do?" Howie asked. "We're just a bunch of kids."

"Maybe we should tell our parents," Liza suggested.

"Nobody would believe us," Melody said. "They'd think we'd gone completely bonkers."

"We've got to think of something," Howie said. "Before it's too late."

"I know what I'm going to do," Eddie interrupted. "I'll prove Mr. O'Grady isn't a leprechaun!"

8

Master Trickster

"I've got it," Eddie said the next morning as Howie, Melody, and Liza met under the oak tree.

"Got what," Melody giggled, "chicken pox?"

"You should get a job with the circus, you're so funny," Eddie snapped.

"Go on," Howie urged, "what were you going to say?"

"I know how to prove Mr. O'Grady isn't a leprechaun!" Eddie said.

"How?" Liza asked.

"If he's a leprechaun, like you think, he'll be able to outtrick me," Eddie explained as he grabbed his bookbag and headed inside.

"Wait!" Melody yelled. "It could be dangerous to make a leprechaun mad!"

But Eddie didn't listen to his friends as they followed him into the school.

"You don't know who you're dealing with," Howie pleaded.

"Mr. Potato Head doesn't know who *he's* dealing with," Eddie snapped as he hung up his jacket in the hallway. "But he'll find out during gym class."

Melody, Liza, and Howie tried to talk to Eddie during class, but Mrs. Jeepers flashed her eyes to silence them. For once, Eddie didn't mind.

Just before gym, Eddie raised his hand. "Yes?" Mrs. Jeepers asked in her strange accent.

"May I please be excused?" Eddie asked as politely as he knew how.

Mrs. Jeepers raised her eyebrows and looked hard at him. But then she slowly nodded her head. "You must hurry. We will be ready to leave for physical education in less than five minutes."

Eddie nodded and rushed out of the

room. He got back just as the class was lining up. Nobody noticed that Eddie was wearing his jacket as he slipped into line between Howie and Liza.

"What are you going to do?" Liza asked with concern.

Eddie patted his bulging jacket pocket. "I'm going to prove that I'm the master trickster!"

The third-graders entered the gym. Mr. O'Grady was standing on the other side of the gym bouncing a basketball. He looked from face to face, but he didn't look in anybody's eyes. "Top of the morning to you," he called. "Won't you be a-joining me for a little game of basketball?"

Eddie beat everybody to the other side of the gym and stood in front of Mr. O'Grady. The little man glanced at Eddie's raised hand.

"What would you be a-wanting?" Mr. O'Grady asked.

Eddie looked at Howie and grinned before he answered Mr. O'Grady. "Can we dance again today?"

"I thought you would rather be a-shooting hoops." Mr. O'Grady glanced around the gym. "But 'twould be a pleasure to be teaching you another Irish jig."

"No," Eddie interrupted. "I want to teach you a dance of *ours.*"

Mr. O'Grady touched the leather pouch hanging from his waistband and gently tugged on the string. "And what might you be a-calling this dance?"

Eddie grinned as he pulled a small jar out of his pocket. "It's called the Honey Bee Waltz," he yelled as he unscrewed the lid. "And it's guaranteed to keep you hopping!" And with that, Eddie lightly rolled the jar toward Mr. O'Grady's feet.

Carey was the first to scream. "Bees! Watch out for the bees!" And then she ran out the door.

The jar broke and honey bees swarmed out and onto Mr. O'Grady's bright red sweat suit.

"Watch out," Liza screamed. "They'll sting you!"

But Mr. O'Grady didn't seem upset at all. Instead he reached into his leather pouch and pulled out the small red stone. One by one, the bees flew away and out the open gym window.

"Wow!" Howie yelled. "How did you do that?"

"To be sure," Mr. O'Grady chuckled, "'twas just a bit of Irish luck. But since you like to dance so much, we'll have another jig tomorrow."

Howie jabbed Eddie. "So much for your Honey Bee Waltz!"

"Shut up," Eddie muttered as he plopped onto the bleachers. It was then that Eddie found out—not all of the honey bees had left.

"Oww!" Eddie jumped up and grabbed

his behind. "I've been stung!"

"Look, everyone," Melody yelled, "Eddie's doing the Honey Bee Waltz."

All the kids laughed as Eddie raced out of the gym.

9

Eddie's War

Eddie wasn't surprised when Principal Davis called him to the office after school. Principal Davis looked like Humpty Dumpty with glasses as he frowned at Eddie.

"Sit down, young man," he said gruffly.

"Do I have to?" Eddie whined.

Principal Davis almost cracked a smile. "Bees are dangerous. They're nothing to play around with."

"I know," Eddie muttered.

"I don't want to catch you misbehaving again," Principal Davis continued. "Let this be a lesson to you. Tricks will get you in the end."

Eddie rubbed his bee sting. "I know," he said again as he left Principal Davis' office.

His friends were waiting for him under the oak tree.

"Now do you believe us?" Melody said. "Mr. O'Grady is the leprechaun after Mrs. Jeepers' Fairy Stone."

"Maybe we should just let him take it," Eddie grumbled.

"No!" Liza shouted. "Mr. O'Grady might hurt Mrs. Jeepers."

Howie shook his head. "Besides, if Mr.

O'Grady got the stone, the world as we know it would end. Leprechauns would be running all over the place tricking people."

"Eddie wouldn't care," Melody told them. "He's always playing tricks anyway."

"He'd never get a chance to play anymore tricks," Howie said. "The leprechauns would take care of that."

Eddie rubbed his sore spot. "You may have a point. We have to do something."

"But what?" Melody cried.

"I have an idea," Howie said quietly. "We have to do what my grandmother said. We've got to make him look us in the eyes. Then he'll do whatever we say."

"How?" Liza squeaked. "Mr. O'Grady doesn't ever look straight at us."

Eddie interrupted. "There's only one way. We have to trick the trickster."

His three friends were quiet.

"How?" Melody finally asked. "You saw what he did when you tried to trick him this morning."

"Gather round," Eddie said, "and I'll tell you."

Liza's eyes grew big as Eddie whispered the plan. "Do you think it'll work?" she asked.

"It's got to," Howie said.

Melody gulped. "All right. Let's do it!"

10

Up to Their Eyeballs in Trouble

The next morning the four friends huddled under the oak tree. "It has to be today," Howie insisted. "Grandma said leprechauns can only leave the Emerald Isle for three days, and this is Mr. O'Grady's third day."

Liza interrupted. "Let's all just leave him alone and let him go back to Ireland."

"We can't," Melody explained. "Mr. O'Grady is bound to make his move to steal the Fairy Stone today."

"We have to stop him before he has the chance," Howie added.

Eddie nodded. "I'll do it today—during gym."

"What will we do until then?" Liza asked.

"Just be normal," Eddie suggested as they went into the room.

But Mrs. Jeepers was not her normal self. Her red hair hung limply around her face, and dark circles were underneath her dull green eyes. Her white blouse was wrinkled and she wasn't wearing her bat bracelet. Even her green brooch seemed to have lost its shine, and she didn't smile her odd little half smile when she said, "Hello, children."

The rest of the morning was strange, too. Mrs. Jeepers jumped at every little noise and her eyes kept darting toward the darkened hallway.

"Mrs. Jeepers seems nervous," Liza whispered.

"I think she's scared," Melody said softly.

"You'd be scared, too," Howie added, "if the future of the world was pinned to your shirt."

Nobody said a word when Mrs. Jeepers

forgot to give the spelling test. Eddie worried that she would forget about gym, too. He almost wished she would, but at 10:30 Mrs. Jeepers sighed and slumped at her desk. "Boys and girls, it is time for physical education. You may walk by yourselves to the gymnasium. I will come for you at the end of the class period."

Then she put her head down on her desk and was quiet.

"I think she's sleeping," Melody said as they tiptoed out of the room.

"I don't like seeing Mrs. Jeepers this way," Liza said softly.

"I'd like it," Eddie admitted, "if it wasn't so weird."

Melody stopped at the gym door. "I'm afraid to go inside."

"We have to," Eddie said.

Howie nodded. "Grandma said the way to capture a leprechaun is to stare at him without blinking. It's the only magic that controls him. Once Eddie has captured him, he'll have to do whatever we say."

"But what if you blink?" Liza worried.

"I don't want to think about that," Eddie shuddered.

"But if you do outstare him, you can get his bag of jewels, *and* make him leave," Howie pointed out.

"You're right. It's now or never." Eddie

gulped and rubbed his eyes with his knuckles before he followed his friends into the gym. Mr. O'Grady was waiting on the other side of the gym by the record player.

Eddie didn't waste any time. He marched right up to Mr. O'Grady and tugged on his red sleeve.

"There's something in my eye," Eddie whined.

Mr. O'Grady turned away and laughed. "To be sure, 'tis nothing but your eyeball."

"Ha, ha," Eddie said without a smile. "But I'm serious, it really hurts. You have to look at it."

Mr. O'Grady shooed Eddie away. "Don't be a-troubling me. I have a dance to be a-teaching." Then he turned on the record player and started dancing to the Irish tune.

Howie nudged Eddie in the back. "Keep trying."

Eddie stepped in front of Mr. O'Grady. "I'll be your partner," he said. But Mr. O'Grady leapt away. Eddie spent the entire gym time chasing his teacher around the hopping third-graders. Eddie was almost ready to give up when he ran smack dab into Mr. O'Grady as he was doing a twirl.

Eddie hopped up and tried to look into Mr. O'Grady's eyes. But Mr. O'Grady was not to be tricked. He reached into his little pouch and sidestepped Eddie.

"Watch out!" Melody squealed. "He has a magic stone."

Eddie jumped back and joined his three friends.

"Why might you be a-thinking I have magic?" Mr. O'Grady asked softly.

"We know who you are," Eddie blurted, "and we know why you're here."

"We're going to stop you," Howie added.

Mr. O'Grady pulled out the small red jewel from his pouch. "'Tis foolish to be a-thinking you can stop me!"

11

Swing Your Partner

Melody gasped when the door swung open and Mrs. Jeepers stepped into the gym.

"We've got to do something!" Melody gasped.

But it was too late. Mr. O'Grady dashed to the door and grabbed Mrs. Jeepers' hands. He started to twirl her around the gym, keeping time to the music.

"Look!" Carey squealed. "Mrs. Jeepers is dancing with Mr. O'Grady." The rest of the kids pointed and laughed. Everybody, that is, except Howie, Liza, Melody, and Eddie. They stared as Mr. O'Grady spun Mrs. Jeepers faster and faster around the gym. Her black shoes flew off the floor, and her long red hair was swept back.

"He's going too fast," Liza cried as she headed for the dancing teachers. "Mrs. Jeepers can't reach her brooch!"

"He's going to snatch it!" Howie warned.

"Not if I can help it," Eddie yelled, following Liza. Just as Mr. O'Grady reached for the sparkling brooch, Eddie dived and grabbed the little man's ankle. Mr. O'Grady went crashing to the floor. Without thinking, Liza plopped on his chest. Mr. O'Grady gasped—and looked straight at the little girl holding him down. Liza stared back at the blue eyes of the wrinkled little man.

"Don't look away!" Howie shouted. "Whatever you do, don't blink!"

Liza took a slow breath, but she kept her eyes on Mr. O'Grady.

"It's working," Melody said from behind her. "He can't take his eyes away."

"Tell him now," Howie added.

Liza nodded. "It's not that we don't like

you, it's just that Mrs. Jeepers was here first. I'm not going to stop staring until you promise to leave her alone—and leave Bailey Elementary."

"So, that's the way it 'tis." Mr. O'Grady winced.

Mrs. Jeepers towered over Mr. O'Grady—and Liza. Her green eyes flashed and she gently rubbed the green brooch at her throat. The stone seemed to glow as she spoke. "The children are correct. A school is not the proper place for your shenanigans." Mrs. Jeepers reached down to help Liza to her feet. Liza glanced at her teacher's outstretched hand.

As soon as Liza looked away, Mr. O'Grady scrambled up. A slow grin spread across his wrinkled face. "The lively jig wasn't meant to be a-causing harm. We folk must dance to live!"

Mrs. Jeepers's eyes flashed at the little man, and then she walked away. The

class fell into line behind her as she left the gym.

Liza squeezed in behind Melody, Howie, and Eddie. "I'm sorry," she whispered. "I didn't mean to look away."

"That's all right," Melody said. "Besides, maybe you stared at him long enough. After all, he was looking at you when you told him to leave."

"I just hope you're right," Howie said softly.

12

The End of the Rainbow

It started to sprinkle shortly before lunch and angry storm clouds dumped sheets of rain during math. Mrs. Jeepers didn't mention her strange dance in gym that morning, but she did seem more cheerful.

The rain slowed to a sprinkle during science, and by the time the bell rang to end the school day, the sun was trying to peep through the clouds. Melody, Liza, Eddie, and Howie stood under the oak tree. Big drops fell from the branches and plopped on their heads.

"Look!" Melody pointed. "A rainbow." Liza, Howie, and Eddie looked to see a full rainbow arching across the sky.

"It's beautiful," Liza said. "I wonder if it really does lead to the Emerald Isle."

"We'll know tomorrow," Howie said, "if Mr. O'Grady is gone."

When Mrs. Jeepers greeted the children the next morning she looked like her regular self. She wore black pointy boots, a black skirt, a starched white lace collar, and her bat bracelet. And at her neck was the sparkling green brooch. Her hair was swept back in a proper ponytail and she smiled her odd little half smile. "Good morning, children. Did you get to see the lovely rainbow yesterday?"

"Yes, it was the biggest rainbow I've ever seen," Melody said.

The rainbow seemed to put everyone in a good mood. Everyone, that is, except Coach Ellison. He nearly growled when the kids got to the gym. "I don't know what you did to Mr. O'Grady, but whatever it was, you made him leave. He left me a note saying he wanted to go back home where it was safe!"

"All right!" Howie slapped Eddie on the back. "We did it!"

"I guess we showed him who the master tricksters are," Eddie bragged.

Liza smiled. "I guess Bailey Elementary isn't big enough for a vampire *and* a leprechaun."

Melody giggled. "I don't think Bailey Elementary is big enough for a leprechaun and *us!*"